FIRST STORY
CHANGING LIVES THROUGH WRITING

First Story changes lives through writing.

There is dignity and power in telling our own story. We help disadvantaged young people find their voices.

First Story places professional writers into secondary schools serving low-income communities, where they work intensively with students and teachers to foster confidence, creativity and writing ability.

Our programmes expand young people's horizons and raise aspirations. Students gain vital skills that underpin their success in school and support their transition to further education and employment.

To find out more and get involved, go to www.firststory.org.uk.

First Story is a registered charity number 1122939 and a private company limited by guarantee incorporated in England with number 06487410. First Story is a business name of First Story Limited.

First published 2019 by First Story Limited
Omnibus Business Centre, 39–41 North Road, London, N7 9DP

www.firststory.org.uk

ISBN 978-0-85748-408-6

1 3 5 7 9 10 8 6 4 2

A CIP catalogue record for this book is available from the British Library.

Printed and bound in the UK by Aquatint
Typeset by Avon DataSet Ltd
Copyedited by Beth Kruszynskyj
Proofread by Gemma Harris
Cover illustrated and designed by Lee Harrison

Afternoon Tea from the Void

An Anthology by the First Story Group
at St Mary's College

EDITED BY LEE HARRISON | 2019

FIRST STORY
CHANGING LIVES THROUGH WRITING

As Patron of First Story I am delighted that it continues to foster and inspire the creativity and talent of young people in secondary schools serving low-income communities.

I firmly believe that nurturing a passion for reading and writing is vital to the health of our country. I am therefore greatly encouraged to know that young people in this school – and across the country – have been meeting each week throughout the year in order to write together.

I send my warmest congratulations to everybody who is published in this anthology.

Camilla

HRH The Duchess of Cornwall

Contents

Introduction

Lee Harrison, Writer-in-Residence

It is a strange time to be a young human on planet Earth. One of the recurring themes of this year's workshops at St Mary's was the idea of *zeitgeist*. When we asked the question – what is the spirit of the times? The consensus seemed to be... we're not really sure.

On reflection though, *not-knowing* is about right. It's okay. Certainty can be a dangerous thing, and in uncertain times, creativity is the best resource. To the writer, the gaping void is just a blank page waiting to be filled. The hardcore writer learns not to panic in the face of doubt, but to sip tea, eat biscuits and work something out.

Being a fantasy writer, I'm a firm believer that the weird, the offbeat, the unlikely – and indeed, the *cats in a bag bonkers* – are useful tools for reflecting. From the refuge of the various elsewheres we create with our writing, we can look back at ourselves and our world in a fresh light.

It's a good job as well. This year the St Mary's Learning Resource Centre hosted a larger, much younger group and the dynamic was that much more energetic. Every week they attacked the tasks I handed out. We wrestled Alligator Pepper. We wrote haiku, revelled in triumph and failure, pain and fear; we vandalised in order to create. Even when, in the final session, the writers were confronted with a dark mastermind, they managed to wrest control of their fates. And along this path, they set about sorting out what their own zeitgeists were up to. And so, I am proud to present for your pleasure, *Afternoon Tea from the Void* – a surprising crop of writing, which, you will find, is in turns surreal, portentous and enigmatic.

I would like to thank my group – it was a right old knees-up to work with you, and every week was an invigorating experience. I was most proud to see the group read and perform at the University of Hull for First Story's Regional Writing Day – and to see one student receive the runner-up prize in the national (*national*, mind) 100-word short story competition. Seeing an event like that really hits home what First Story does.

I shall also extend thanks to Miss Roberts and Mrs Bedworth, who, after three years, remain the glue that holds the whole thing together. They do so with genuine enthusiasm, and it was an especial pleasure, after a prolonged absence last year, to have Miss Roberts back with a twinkle in her literacy-coordinating eye. This year we were joined by new recruit Mr Gouldson, who took to the role with a pleasing sense of mischief, even acting as a life model at one point – with his clothes on, obviously. Safeguarding is paramount.

The times they are a-changin', and the empty page is a void. But that's alright – make a cup of tea and fill it.

Foreword

Miss H. Roberts, Whole School Literacy Coordinator, and Mr M. Gouldson, First Story Lead Teacher

2019 has been a year of growth and excitement within the St Mary's First Story camp. We welcomed back Lee Harrison as our official Writer-in-Residence for the school programme and, as always, he brought a unique, perpetual flavour of niche originality, the fruits of which are found within the pages you are about to unearth. The roots of our ideas flourished with Lee's careful cultivation and, as you will see, the students rooted themselves steadfastly in his imaginative paradise.

For the first time, we officially opened up the programme to our school's seedlings and this brought a whole new dynamic of eccentricity to the workshops Lee led and managed. Two years on from City of Culture and our students are clearly still reaping the benefits from programmes like First Story, which allow them to blossom into confident, creative individuals whose writing has delved into the deepest parts of their imaginations.

As lead teachers, it has been a pleasure to watch these students grow and come to fruition, from our nervous initial meeting to the final flourish as they handed in their completed work. We could not be prouder of our budding writers and their wonderful off-the-wall take on life and its many predicaments. Their constant enthusiasm and *joie de vivre* make staying after school, following a day of teaching, a joy, and Tuesday afternoons will never be the same; the absence of Lee's weekly offerings in the form of various sweet treats will be particularly missed!

Over the sixteen sessions, we have considered our heroes, awakened our senses and turned the ordinary firmly on its head.

The students have freely explored around our LRC different ways and modes of writing under the watchful eye of our all-knowing Overlord. They have always participated, frequently challenged and unreservedly contributed to this fantastic collection of literary blooms, each piece an integral petal of quirky beauty.

We at St Mary's College would like to thank, once again, everyone at First Story and NCOP Humber Region who have made our anthology and its production possible. We have seen friendships be made and thrive throughout the creative process, through collaborative work, as well as through sharing ideas and stories. And not to mention the wealth of opportunities Lee's workshops and First Story events have brought, enhancing the students' creativity and nurturing a positive relationship with writing.

We sincerely hope you enjoy the harvest of the students' success and that you relish every delicious morsel from our *Afternoon Tea from the Void*.

I Stabbed my Sister with a Fork

Faith Doyle

Seizing my little pink kazoo
My sister's taunting laughter
Cheshire-Cat grins and greyhound stature
Beat me down like I'm the runt.
I *am* the runt.
A sour rot lingered in my chest.
The fork glinted on the table
I saw small stubby fingers reaching for it
As if they weren't my own
One swift motion
Her laughter choked into a scream
The stately greyhound became a yelping chihuahua.
The fork clattered to the ground.
I was done for.
I wondered
If that little pink kazoo
Was worth it.

The Last Moment

Bishop Fintan

At the last moment…
Cut the blue or the red?
Select a wire.
Cut.
Time stopped.
I was a cobra dancing before I went for the bite
I was Armstrong about to land on the moon
Taking glory and fame in my hands
I was a surgeon
Poised over a bullet
Lodged in a soldier's head
I was a mouse getting closer to the smell of cheese

The timer bleeped
Countdown resumed.
My last moment.
I was Superman falling from a Kryptonite sky
I was a slug eroded by salt flakes
I was a book, half-read and abandoned
I was a bird, shamed by my conflict with a window
I was a white pencil crayon waiting to be used
As space, time and vision drifted away.

The last moment.

Alligator Pepper

Daniel Adeniji

The alligator struck with a bloodthirsty bite.
After that, my tongue was set alight.
My friends laughed at me.
I said this isn't right.
I think me and this pepper are having a fight.
It wasn't just my face that went tight.
Something tells me
I won't be sleeping tonight.

Kim Kardashian's Butt

Deanna Gay

I am Kim Kardashian's butt
My plump, luscious life
Blessed with an A-M-A-Z-I-N-G lifestyle.
My plumpness numbs out negativity
Or sympathy.
Any feelings at all.
A lot of people love me
Copycats try to be just like me
But they're delirious.
Because when Kimmy eventually passes away
When the world is a smoking ruin
I'll still be there
A household name.
My circular, glutinous mass
Forever a stamp in history.

Cheerio

Ellen Shepherdson

I remember running down the stairs that day. The clean, fluffy carpet under my feet. Nutella on toast. The sweet smell of early morning tea.

I had ten minutes before I had to leave for school. Just enough time for a bowl of Cheerios. I barely noticed my dad, approaching gingerly. Worry lining his face. I stopped mid-crunch.

He was struggling to find his words. To tell the truth. Why had he left so abruptly in the middle of the night?

I remembered Grandpa.

Despondent, I looked down at the bowl of honey-glazed treats, now sinking beneath the milk.

Cheerio.

Peppercorn

Stanley Vickers

Fiery hell scorching my mouth.
Tiny devils of spice
Poking my tongue with their tridents
Twisted dragons blistering my throat
Tongues of fire bubbling in my stomach
A million greedy chillies snatching the breath from my lungs.
Rioters burning my tongue with their torches.

I gulped a glass of cold fresh milk
And felt the demons melt away.
A patrol of knights charging the devils
Soothing fighter-jets shooting down the dragons
Firefighters dousing the riot of spice.

A Fragrant Nowhere

Faith Doyle

I pick my date up in my old Nissan Juke. It rattles for the entirety of the journey, but we manage to laugh it off. The dusk sky glows, the conversation flows, and things are going okay. She says she enjoys spicy foods – and has brought grains of paradise.

To impress her, I stuff three in my mouth. The intense spice rears like a volcano, and I swerve off the road into a field of lavender. We plough through, screaming, and are left stunned in the middle of a fragrant nowhere.

And to top it off, my mouth is still burning.

Paintbrush

Gracie Chapman

Heaven stopped
So that my passion,
My paintbrush,
Drew a soul in the silence

Banger

Joyel James

I approached the pitch,
Nerves jangling inside of me,
Urging my breakfast out,
More nervous now
Than on my first day at school.

Last two minutes.
Two–nil down
Then I got the ball.
I didn't know what to do.
Shoot! Came the cries.
I took a huge swing.
It rocketed out
Then curled in.
GOAL!!
Everyone jumped onto me
And all I remember
Is that, to be fair –
It really was a banger.

Lavender

Alfie Lansdell

Lavender must die
Slowly, the deadly scent
Spears me in the nose
Pesky purple poisons my heart
Harpoons my chest
Lavender is a thunderstorm
A lighting strike
While I am the lame earth
Lavender spitfires shoot
Fragrant bullets
Waging war on my nostrils
Lavender, what did I do to hurt you?
As I fall, it takes its final blow
I take my last bow
I die

Amelia the Party Crasher

Amelia Szuma

Although I've only been to a few parties
I've seen people come in their buggafies
I walk onto the floor
And make the crowd roar
They have no answer
Such a bad dancer
I rely on my skills
My dancing kills
I crash bad parties
And make them more hearty
Yeah! That's my name:
Amelia the Party Crasher.

Gouldson

Class Poem

Gouldson is many things.
He is a floral, fancy-pants fashionista
An anachronistic anteater asleep at the wheel
Sinister, like a slithering snake
An insidious iguana

Isolated in iridescent imaginings
Gouldson's thoughts clamour like a catastrophic catfight
He is stone-faced, like an ancient statue lost in the folds of time
A brooding hate, trapped by its own passion

Gouldson's frothing facial hair frolicks like a furry ferret
Devious, devilish, darling eyes darken diabolically
Sinister as a slick sorcerer
He is a mysterious monstrosity of magic

Gouldson is anomalous, like an ant all alone
A prehistoric pink piranha
Cannibalistic, like a capering caveman
A diabolical, dangerous dinosaur

Gouldson is sinister, like a secretive spy
Strong like a stationary soldier
Plum, like a purple-painted princess
Peaceful like a private puppy

Pig on a Windowsill

Lailanna Lawson

I was sweating like a pig on a windowsill
I was standing on the stage
Everyone was staring at me
The weight was pushing me down, breaking my back
Everyone was staring at me
Like starving diners waiting for Sunday dinner
Like a noob in last place on Battle Royale
Like Doge with No Wow

Then I opened my mouth.
All I did was open my mouth
And glorious tunes began to flow out
The crowd came back, chanting my name.
I was full Doge with SO MUCH WOW

I Would Like to Write

Lordrine Owusu

I would like to write myself
Into the job of US President.
I would like to write a novel
That will drag people out of their world
That will show the way
Between the heavens and earth
Between drama and comedy.
I would like to write something
That will make your mind say STOP!
That will bring world peace.

I Am Batman

Lucy Cook

My black cloak hasn't been washed in years.
I take down villains with my violent armpit smell.
I can't wait to get out there.
I am like chocolate spread waiting to be smeared around
    the toast.

When I found out they were making a movie about me,
I thought I'd better wash my cloak.
Be more hygienic.
I found myself waiting in line to get the tickets for my movie.
People staring.
I am so scared.

I make up an excuse to leave.
I say –
I am Batman.
I have dirty work to do.
And I am proud of it.

Open Your Eyes

Luka Coenen

Open your eyes
Let the exotic lights consume you
The alligator lies
The paradise promised is not true
Open your eyes.
Sweet scents of lavender fill your lungs
The pain burns but you're not done
You can hear the triumph of the songs
Over the hillside you can almost see the sun

Letter from Chuck

Stanley Vickers

Dear Sir,

I am disappointed by the performance of these so called 'action jeans' as they did not allow me to do a high-kick, nor to take out a tank using nothing but a sandwich toaster. In fact, they split upon opening the packet. I was highly irritated as the package did not come with a wig, or even a moustache, and I had already bought myself a blowtorch for shaving.

Yours angrily,
Carlos Ray Norris

Homeworld Dystopia

Alfie Lansdell and Luka Coenen

My zeitgeist lives in a homeworld dystopia
Wearing torn, second-hand clothes
Fighting every day
With a useless sword
Passed down through generations
My zeitgeist has no pet dog
He fears dying and being forgotten
Hoping to one day expand his empire
Eating home-grown seeds
His body is made of light
He forgets himself

Never-Ending Paradise

Amelia Szuma and Lordrine Owusu

When I sank my teeth into the pepper, it was a moment of joy and sorrow. It was as if I had fallen into a never-ending hole that surrounded me with hot fire. I could see the lifeless people who had gone through this torture. I could see my future already: Satan, seizing me by the collar, spitting acid on my face and laughing his head off.

Until that horrible flavour stripped off my tongue.

Then, it was as if an angel came to sweep me up in a bright flash of blinding light. It was magical. An angel, dressed in a bleached white robe, with big angel wings and a bright yellow halo on top of his head.

Am I in heaven? Am I dreaming? One million questions flooded my mind.

Or am I dead? Are you God? Are you real?

Zeitgeist

Bishop Fintan

The greatest enemy of my Zeitgeist is a locked door. He lives in a normal house, wearing a bland pantsuit of blubbering black. He has no friends, no family, and nothing to care about. He doesn't eat. He spends hours just staring out of the window, waiting for something to happen. It is always raining. Sometimes he wishes someone would kill him painlessly.

There are times when he hears strange sounds from outside and wants to go and find out what made them. But he remembers the locked door. He is a master of all fighting styles and weapons. He *is* a weapon. His dreams are full of adventure and action. Romance and comedy. Of living an adventure, rather than dreaming one.

But he cannot knock down that door.

Greyhound

Daniel Adeniji

It was the last sun-hazed day of the holidays and the thought
    of school loomed.
I was a bright strawberry that was about to rot
I was Didier Drogba ready to come off after the last match
A shaken can of pop that was about to burst
A greyhound about to go into retirement

Ombré

Deanna Gay

Light, beyond porcelain clouds, fills the sky,
Beaming down on vermilion flowers;
A streak through the air,
A paint-stroke from cerise to cyan.
The warming scent drifts past,
Leaves, like graceful fairies, flutter by,
Dancing towards the horizon.
Evergreen trees loom
Swaying from side to side
I felt a droplet of water run down my arm.
And then another.
Again and again.
Until howling, attacking rain broke loose.
A beautiful field turned into a drenched mass.
Ruined, gone, never to be witnessed again.

Cafe Generation

Ellen Shepherdson

It was the purest reflection of a Sunday morning
Glazed in summer-scene-sheen
The orange-painted walls
Played host to the collective memories
Of a fallen generation.
Spending hours soaking up the sun's vicious light
Without a care for what might happen tomorrow
Chatting away to each other
Remnants of this glorious age
Humming gently to the playful tunes
That resound from the Sixties songs on the radio.

I Want to Rant

Faith Doyle

I want to write a major existential crisis
I want to write heartbreaking tragedies
I want to write a cookbook
On a desk. In a submarine.
The screams and panics at the end of the world.
I want to write the ghosts who watch us all the time
And compress human life into the form of a West End show
    for aliens.
I want to reveal that we are all aliens.
I want to write the suffering of a miserable lifetime.
I want to spread paranoia and uncertainty for the future.
I want to write a world in which people are walked by animals
Where we're all fluent in chipmunk
And forced to eat cat food and dog food
Whilst the animals who suffered eating such revolting stuff
Can comfortably enjoy our misery.
I want to write the brainwashing of animals
Being brainwashed by Mr Gouldson
Who's being brainwashed by Theresa May
To make him do her bidding.
I want to write a tentacled paranoia that wrings out your lungs,
That dices your emotions and leaves them to die from frostbite
With no way of thawing.
I want to write something nasty that pops out of the blue.
A train, nowhere near the tracks
That falls out of the sky on the way to school
Death by sixteen spears
By one thousand baseballs

By liquefication
By buttering-up
By frying
I want to write the only time that will tell.
I think I'm the one
Having a major existential crisis.

A Volley of Haiku

Gracie Chapman

Drip, drop, down it goes
Disappears down the hole
The sink has it now

*

Ruffle of dark fur
Tail flicking repeatedly
A cat's anger builds

*

Haikus make nonsense
Not all the time, like this one
Wait, that makes no sense

*

Coffee or tea? Which?
The silent war of ages
Will it ever end?

*

Five syllables here
Look! Here's another seven
I wrote a haiku

Babies

Joyel James

Babies and toddlers
And their immature brains
Research the parents.

In an emergency situation
Such as a fair, a sports day or dance
You can borrow them for a short time.

The library stamps them
You must bring them back on time.

BLAZEFUR

Lailanna Lawson

My Zeitgeist is a mix of dragon and cat called BLAZEFUR. It has no gender and lives in a galactic cave in another universe, where it wears a black T-shirt and navy jeans, and plays on a games console all day every day. My Zeitgeist is afraid of clowns and dolls and wants to be the best singer in the world. BLAZEFUR has a bow and arrow, can turn into a wolf, and sometimes eats slugs.

Tea

Lordrine Owusu

Lordrine really wants some tea.
He shouted and shouted
But he doubted
If he would get his tea.
A bee flew past and Lordrine asked
Can he have some tea?
In search of the lost time
The distinguished thought of a cup of tea
Lingers and disturbs
And Lordrine thinks – 'I feel most free when I drink
    magnificent tea.'
His fingers and toes feel like they are falling off.

Apocalypse Sandwich

Lucy Cook

Peach-coloured bread sat on top of the lonely ham
I saw my boyfriend and *bam*
'I'm sorry,' I said, 'I just hate mayo,'
I left feeling bad
And him feeling sad

I ate my sandwich feeling empty
The world was a dark thundercloud
The rain scattered amongst dark, sorry faces
Homes had transformed to war trenches
Trees became mushroom clouds
The emergency services were overwhelmed

At the darkest hour
He came back with it
Another sandwich.
This time, tuna and cheese.

Zeitgeist

Luka Coenen

My Zeitgeist cowers, hidden behind a barrier of hatred
His face unrecognised
His opinion unheard
Not able to speak a single word
Caged off by the thoughts of others
Searching for help in an empty field

Whatever Happened to Barry Scott?

Stanley Vickers

Bang! After the dirt was gone, Barry Scott moved away. Nowadays, Barry loiters by a mountain spring in the heart of Indonesia. He has a cold and rasping voice like nails on a chalkboard, and smells like day-old fish and mountain dew. He has no family and friends, apart from diving birds. He sends these birds to do his bidding; shoplifting and mugging rich people. At the end of the day, he uses an old sponge he found in the river to clean his thieving birds. He secretly believes the birds are women. He has a crush on one of them. He longs for unlimited power and a sandwich toaster.

In the Darkness of the Lavatory

Bishop Fintan

My stomach felt like a balloon as I tugged on the doorknob. It
felt like I had just died standing in the darkness of the lavatory.
Joy turned into pain
Pain turned into anguish
Anguish turned into fear
Fear turned into complete terror
Complete terror turned into boredom
Then irritation,
As I started wondering what was for tea.

Clearer Image

Daniel Adeniji

In fortunate countries
Like England or Sweden
Lip-readers attempt to process
The magic of the local authorities
For a clearer image

A World of Colour

Ellen Shepherdson

I am the old book, waiting behind a shelf, a shelf full of new
    and better books
I was a shadow in a crowd of people
I was an innocent voice waiting to be heard
I was a soldier, stationary in a stance
I was a shade of black in a world of colour
I was the ugly duckling in a pond full of swans
I was the fat girl in a room crammed with models
I was the last option that no one wanted
It was just a normal day

Suddenly a small, sticky hand grabbed my spine.
A quick, static shock electrocuted its way through my pages
For once –
I was a rainbow in the storm
I was the man singing in the rain
I was the skyscraper towering over the people below
I was the helium balloon floating high in the sky
I was the treasure hidden at the bottom of the sea
I was the star of my own Broadway show

The sensation I had long forgotten came rushing back.
It was the feeling that made my spine tingle
And my words feel fuzzy.
I am the old book, no longer waiting on the shelf
Behind stories I once thought were better than mine.

Northern Lights

Gracie Chapman

Northern lights flood the sky
The flutter of an owl flying by
Scent of flowers, freshly cut
Their lingering smell easing my foot
The pain comes again, as cold as fire
The black illness creeping higher and higher
They call this paradise
It's more like a hell
A nightmare in disguise
Shells fly by, forcing me back
Into the bustling street
I felt for my gun.
Took the shot, got ready to go
Bustled in my pocket
Looking for one small thing
A small white pill
Down the hatch
The small orb sat on my tongue
As I chomped down, I heard a scream
Convulsing on the floor lay a comrade
I stood, observing, not feeling any pain
Like watching a war from the battlefronts
Closed my eyes, took a deep breath
Terrorists have a price to pay, I guess
Waiting for the dark wave of death
That never came.

The Ballad of Joyel James

Joyel James

Football is a game
Where the ball is the battle
Winning is the way

Life is a hard war
Between you and your mindset
Happy mind is happy life

No worries around, only happiness
Balloons lifting like a plastic bag
This is life, calm and steady

Extreme Eyes

Lucy Cook

Extreme eyes have been classifying data since the dawn of time
Each animal has a role
Gazelles code humans
Whilst horseshoe crabs try to host them
While humans mutate
This task becomes harder
Until humans spread into every habitat
Soon, animals would no longer exist
But they take their chance to take back the world
Trees start to arise
Planes drop from the sky
Thunder and lightning genocide
For all evolved apes
The end was approaching

I Want to Write

Luka Coenen

I want to write an epic fantasy series with no care for continuity
A tale that can take you to the northern hemisphere of your
    imagination
To write myself out of school early
Into a dream job
In Dubai
Where I will write the adventures of Bob, the imaginary man
    in my wardrobe.

I Am Falling

Stanley Vickers

I am falling from a plane whilst eating a mango cheesecake.
I come from Mars, where children rule and adults are enslaved
    by chickens and other types of poultry.
I stand on a crocodile's tail, watching it get indigestion from
    eating green flamingos.
I am sitting in a residential home being force-fed mashed-up
    roast dinner with pills.
I am listening to birds singing, telling me that I have limited
    time to live.

Dystopia

Bishop Fintan

Missing people
Machines not working
Phones are going crazy

No one taking the calls
Broken buildings
Survivors look suddenly older

In newsflashes –
A light in the background
A bird, a flying figure

Near a beach
Over the water
The figure is flying

Light-Headed

Deanna Gay

My Zeitgeist lives next door. All day they just study and exercise, wearing cute pastel colours, stroking dogs and cute pets. They are afraid of making a fool of themselves, or coming across as weird. They hope to become a heart surgeon so as not to disappoint their parents. Most of the time though, they don't really care. They eat Pot Noodles and cereal, and often feel light-headed.

Tiger's Meat

Ellen Shepherdson

From a distance, its elegance beams
Prowling calmly, treading ever so softly
Don't be fooled by its beauty
All it takes is a subtle change in the wind
A delayed reaction.
With a kick of sinewy hind legs
The beast fills your vision,
Amber fur and jade eyes
It is upon you

With a surprising twist.
Claws infiltrate your lungs
A strong, heart-wrenching musk
A grip to maul at your bones.
Never wander too close
Never gaze at its fire-painted fur for more than a second
Never underestimate the deceiving power of beauty
Or you'll end up a tiger's meat.

Schadenfreude

Faith Doyle

Schadenfreude spits in the faces
Of those who look down on her
Whilst choking on tears.
Laughing a deviously merry laugh
Sobbing her heart out.
Every cruel remark she's heard stabs into salt wounds
But she shows no mercy when it's her time to shine.
Wearing a mask of lies,
Schadenfreude sees clearly through paper smiles and blindfolds
To the harsh reality of the world.

Orb

Gracie Chapman

Dim

Faint click

A small whirr.

Flickering to life

Lifeless orb waking up

Illuminated bright patterns

Twirling in a ballroom dance

Like northern lights across the sky

Ribbons soaring across a stage

Slowing down in slovenly coils

Illumination escaping

Fading from view

A small whirr.

Faint click

Dim

Haiku

Lucy Cook

From the dark forests
Pandas roam around, waiting
For a solution

*

How to make dumplings
In just seven easy steps
Roll them cook them done

*

Food is black and white
I devour it thrice a year
Dozing on the bank

*

Angel of darkness
Please answer my pleas and cries
My life is at risk

*

Life, calmly sleeping
Many see its dreams
Now time to wake

*

Why does my boob hurt?
It's a common stage of life
Why doesn't it stop?

*

My heart starts to drown
Why doesn't my mum love me?
I really love her

*

OK, she loves me!
As she kisses me goodnight
My heart is restored

John Smith

Luka Coenen

The room fell silent
Hung on the wall like a coat
The body of John Smith

Balloon

Luka Coenen

The lifespan of a balloon
From inflation – a festival of joy
To the slow descent – when life was lonely
All the while,
Staring the spiky metal fence in the eye

Writer-in-Residence

Bishop Fintan

From the depths of a face
Making mean look meaner
The menace brows again

Shadow

Bishop Fintan

A shadow of nothing
Reminiscent of a boy
Gone, yet to be found

The Power of Words

Lucy Cook

By the power of words vested in me, I shall write magnificent
    fantasy, so the beasts don't come alive and eat me.
I shall write the recipe to exterminate all the non-recyclers
And restore the oceans.
I shall write the magic spell to end world hunger.
I shall shrink problems into specks of dust
Which fly away and disintegrate into air.

Grow Up

Faith Doyle

Tell me to grow up
Just one more time, I dare you
I won't stop crying

The Window of Opportunity

Lucy Cook

I was staring out of the window of opportunity
In my palace of delight
Wearing a cloak of fulfilled dreams
I set off
Dreams were flapping everywhere
Pandas eating bamboo
Our mission:
To make world peace a thing
Filled up on spiritually hopeful cereal
Hoping to fill the world with love
Our mission was paused
For the triceratops of despair and agony had arrived
Time to unleash my weapon:
The hurricane of hope
It was my time to shine

Headless

Amelia Szuma

My friend told me a joke, and I laughed so much my head rolled off. We could never find it again. It was so funny it gave me permanent stitches.

My head is now a non-stop laughing hyena. I don't think it has a pause button. And when I try to get to sleep, it decides to roll over and stay with me.

I awake to my laughing head, looking me straight in the eyes, and laughing.

Tea Void

Ellen Shepherdson

My Zeitgeist lingers in the void
The void of tea that lingers
In the hearts of our fellow British people
With a teapot
Pouring zombies
Into a distinguished nowhere

Six-Word Stories

My outlook on life: never again

Greedy people always die of starvation
Stanley Vickers

Silence can say everything or nothing

Sweet melody corrupted by the lyrics

Amber swish. White flash. Gone again

Silence; a bite. Float violently snatched
Gracie Chapman

I messed up: currently laughing awkwardly

Looks like we've a see-saw homicide

The craziest people are actually sane

Teachers downing coffee like its vodka
Faith Doyle

King overthrown, kills cousin, regains title
Luka Coenen

Trying to avoid possibilities of responsibility
Bishop Fintan

Pokémon. More Pokémon. Eat. Sleep. Memes.

School is hell. I'm behind bars.
Lailanna Lawson

Survive. Kill. Drink. Bandage. Emote. Win.
Alfie Lansdell

School is a pit of lava
Lucy Cook

What a banger – oops. Oh no.

See river. Rod. Bait. Fish. Repeat.
Daniel Adeniji

People don't know that I'm mysterious
Amelia Szuma

Answers for Babies

Lailanna Lawson

Across the seventeen icy wastes and waters
The rooks abandon the rookery
And circle the pack,
Riding with partners
To find answers for babies

The President's List

Faith Doyle

I become the president.
I'm dead
I'm asleep
I'm drawing
I'm hungry
I'm crying
I'm screaming
I'm singing

I'm tired
I'm on my phone
I'm falling
I'm jumping
I'm dreaming
I'm away from home

It's a bad day
We're gonna die
It's not fair
I'm probably hallucinating
Today sucks

We're all dead inside
Maybe we're birds
It would be a paradox
If Pinocchio said
'My nose will grow now'

Biographies

Daniel Adeniji describes himself as friendly, hard-working, happy, careful, caring, handsome, bold and humble. As if that wasn't enough, he also has a knack for writing in rhyme. Legit.

Gracie Chapman is a blazing empress of haiku-like short-form poetry, who can raise whole mountain ranges with a swift stroke of her pen. She is an aspiring artist who can switch from image to word and back again. She is fond of pangolins and recently lost her heart to a primordial terrier. Never ask her to draw hands.

Luka Coenen is a taciturn creature in his natural habitat. He describes himself as an elegant yet sophisticated creature, whose sole purpose... is to kill! But we can tell from his fanciful and sometimes touching turns of phrase that he is a big softy really.

Lucy Cook, panda-tamer and food-devourer, emerged from Hull Royal Infirmary some time ago with work to do. Despite the offbeat tone of her writings, Lucy has a real talent for finding a poignant theme or turn of phrase. She is passionate about recycling and the environment to a near vengeful degree.

Faith Doyle is a scarcely contained vault of words, hailing from a dynasty of fearless warrior writer women. Resplendent with obscure Manga references, she claims to be 'a UTAUloid and a giant weebo, fluent in the weeb language (*Konichiwa watashi wa Doyle Faith – Doiru Feisu-Ohayo! Baka-des! Sumi was SEN, Vickers-san!*).' Faith has a seven-year-old gremlin sister who she force-feeds lemons and kazoos.

Having started life as a pugilistic superhero in Peppa Pig pants, BISHOP FINTAN has since become something of a young philosopher, and writes with a slightly mischievous brand of introspection. Bishop is ever-vigilant about the terms and conditions of biscuit sponsorship deals.

The enigma that is DEANNA GAY seems to be quietly spoken, and yet can be seen performing to packed-out lecture theatres in a crass American accent. Deanna describes herself as 'just your average, stereotypical Asian girl who needs to become a heart surgeon, living in a white cul-de-sac in Hull.' Her writing is distinct for the dark turns it tends to take.

In the beginning, bright light with happiness. In the end, darkness and destruction. In the middle, a boy; his name is JOYEL JAMES, a writer who handles words like the newly arrived gunslinger in a no-good tin-top town. Joyel enjoys football, and is known for his monumental wonder-goals.

ALFIE LANSDELL is a talkative writer with a penchant for obscure statistics. He has a fervent dislike of lavender, which he has learned to confront with his writing. Alfie once walked into a lamp-post at the Houses of Parliament, and is an irrepressible fan of *Doctor Who*.

LAILANNA LAWSON has vast power beyond her size. Also claiming the pseudonyms Sci-Mind and Master of Meat, she is a food-loving, meme-mad girl who loves creative pursuits. Her favourite genres are adventure and horror. She is also very weird and so are most of the people she knows. She loves anime and animals. Lailanna is currently working on a series called 'Ninjamals'.

LORDRINE OWUSU is a free-spirited writer who will one day set the world to rights. He enjoys performing his work, and is a wizard with a whiteboard marker. Lordrine really, *really* wants a cup of tea.

ELLEN SHEPHERDSON pens thoughtfully planned narratives that can paint a whole world in a paragraph. A passionate lover of Bakewell tarts, Ellen is an everyday kind of introvert from Hull with an unhealthy obsession with musical theatre and green tea. She plans to convince the Government to implement a tea-and-biscuits break that is to be held every day. This will, of course, be mandatory.

AMELIA SZUMA is a resilient writer who enjoys dark and supernatural themes, and is a product of her own lavish and thriving imagination. Amelia enjoys subverting social events with her own special brand of dance moves.

To STANLEY VICKERS, the blank page is an invitation to pluck parcels of oddness from the tombola that is his mind. Stanley describes himself as a hopeless child who spends his time desperately wandering around the cultured streets of Hull, whilst he aspires to slay the mighty basilisk. Stanley does not approve of Cristiano Ronaldo.

ACKNOWLEDGEMENTS

Melanie Curtis at Avon DataSet for her overwhelming support for First Story and for giving her time in typesetting this anthology.

Lee Harrison for illustrating and designing the cover of this anthology.

David Greenwood and Foysal Ali at Aquatint for printing this anthology at a discounted rate.

HRH The Duchess of Cornwall, Patron of First Story.

Thanks to:
Arts Council England, Alice Jolly & Stephen Kinsella, Andrea Minton Beddoes & Simon Gray, The Arvon Foundation, BBC Children in Need, Beth & Michele Colocci, Blackwells, Boots Charitable Trust, Brunswick, Charlotte Hogg, Cheltenham Festivals, Clifford Chance, Dulverton Trust, Edith Murphy Foundation, First Editions Club Members, First Story Events Committee, Frontier Economics, Give A Book, Ink@84, Ivana Catovic of Modern Logophilia, Jane & Peter Aitken, John Lyon's Charity, John Thaw Foundation, Miles Trust for the Putney & Roehampton Community, Old Possum's Practical Trust, Open Gate Trust, Oxford University Press, Pscyle Interactive, Royal Society of Literature, Sigrid Rausing Trust, The Stonegarth Fund, Teach First, Tim Bevan & Amy Gadney, Walcot Foundation, Whitaker Charitable Trust, William Shelton Education Charity, XL Catlin, our group of regular donors, and all those donors who have chosen to remain anonymous.

Most importantly we would like to thank the students, teachers and writers who have worked so hard to make First Story a success this year, as well as the many individuals and organisations (including those who we may have omitted to name) who have given their generous time, support and advice.